THE WHALE IS GIGANTIC—FOUR TIMES NORMAL SIZE!

Before the gargantuan mammal can crash into the ship, Bruce emerges from a nearby cabin as Batman. He secures his Bat-Rope to the ship's rigging, and swings far out over the whale and comes down hard on its blowhole with the heel of his foot. *"That should hurt him,"* thinks Batman. *"It's a sensitive spot."* But the whale feels nothing! It keeps plowing through the water toward the terrified passengers on the cruise ship. Batman begins punching the whale's blowhole with his fists. *"Ouch!"* he cries. *"My blows don't even dent this whale blubber!"* The whale opens its mighty jaws and passes along the ship, swallowing a dozen millionaires!

If Batman swings back onto the ship, turn to page 64.

If he swings down inside the whale's mouth, turn to page 50.

Also available from Archway Paperbacks

BATMAN*:

RICHARD WENK

ILLUSTRATED BY JOSÉ DELBO

AN ARCHWAY PAPERBACK
Published by POCKET BOOKS
New York   London   Toronto   Sydney   Tokyo   Singapore

AN ARCHWAY PAPERBACK *Original*

An Archway Paperback published by
POCKET BOOKS, a division of Simon & Schuster Inc.
1230 Avenue of the Americas, New York, NY 10020

ISBN: 0-671-68312-8

First Archway Paperback printing August 1986

17 16 15 14 13 12 11 10 9 8

Printed in the U.S.A.

IL 3+

FOR ELAINE WARING

Attention!

Super Powers Which Way Books must be read in a special way. *Do not read the pages in order.* If you do, the story will make no sense at all. Instead, follow the directions at the bottom of each page until you come to an ending. Only then should you return to the beginning and start over again, making different choices this time.

In this book, *you* make the decisions for Batman. Some of your choices might lead to victory for the Caped Crusader, others to defeat or doom. Of course, Batman would *always* make the correct choices to defeat the villains and save the day, but here, *you* control the Caped Crusader. His fate is in *your* hands! Good luck!

"*What?!*" cries Batman, nearly crashing the Batmobile. He has been speeding toward the dark streets of Gotham on his way to Police Headquarters, when the familiar Bat-Signal suddenly changed into a grinning skull! *Someone has tampered with the searchlight*, thinks Batman. *But why turn the bat silhouette into a DEATH'S HEAD?! It must be a warning . . . or a trap.*

Batman's next move could be critical. A wrong decision might mean his DOOM!

If Batman drives straight to Police Headquarters, turn to page 17.

If he radios Commissioner Gordon from the Batmobile, turn to page 26.

If he plays it safe and uses a public phone, turn to page 3.

For more information on the Bat-Signal, turn to page 119.

This detour road is leading nowhere fast, thinks Batman as he squints to see the dark road ahead. He pulls over and gets out. As soon as he takes two steps, a heavy net is thrown over him! He struggles valiantly, but he is hopelessly entangled—Batman is trapped!

" 'Welcome to my parlor,' said the spider to the bat!" laughs a familiar voice. "You escaped my trick phone booth, but you won't escape this! Ha ha!"

"You're making a mistake," says Batman from the net. "I'm not Batman. . . . Some kid gave me ten dollars to dress up like this and drive the Batmobile."

"What?!" screams the furious voice. "You mean that *punk* tried to dupe *me?* Release this imposter, men!" No sooner is the net removed than Batman leaps into action, rounding up the gang and capturing the Joker.

"It looks like this time the joke was on *you,* Joker!" laughs Batman.

The End

Suspecting a wiretap on his phone, Batman slams on the brakes and rushes to the nearest pay phone. *Hmmm,* he muses, dialing the phone. *This street's unusually deserted . . .*

Suddenly, he hears the Batmobile taking off! With a loud TWANG, the phone booth door locks shut. There is a hissing sound, and the booth begins to fill with white smoke. "Poison gas!" gasps Batman. "Only enough air left for one stunt—!"

If Batman kicks out the glass door, turn to page 24.

If he pulls himself above the rising gas, turn to page 16.

Batman leaps without thinking into a dark corner of the room. "Wrong corner!" roars the Joker, rolling with laughter as he emerges from the other side of the room. "Oh! Ha ha! Such a bad *guess!*" screams the Joker, as his men pin Batman to the wall and tie him to a pipe. "You fool!" laughs the Joker, turning the valve on the steel tank, and rushing out the door. "Somebody might happen to stop by and turn off the gas, but don't hold your breath!" calls the Joker. "Ooh! That joke was a GAS!! Ha! Ha! Ha!"

As he loses consciousness for the last time, Batman hears the Contemptible Clown howling with laughter in the night, and nearby the hissss of escaping gas . . .

The End

At the Gotham *Gazette* offices, Batman discovers all of the night staff tied up in a broom closet! The second edition has already hit the streets with a new headline: GOTHAM CITY TO BE DESTROYED IN 24 HOURS!—THE JOKER! The article beneath states that unless Batman can solve the mystery, the Joker will somehow POISON half the city's population! *How can you poison millions of people in only 24 hours?* wonders Batman desperately. He can think of only three possible ways. *About half the city cooks with gas stoves; everybody drinks city water; and everybody breathes the air. Which is most likely?*

If Batman rushes to the gasworks, turn to page 14.

If he heads for the Gotham Reservoir, turn to page 33.

If he drives to the airport, turn to page 7.

Batman runs into the cabin and starts up the engine, turning the wheel sharply to port. Since the big boat is anchored, it immediately begins speeding around in a tight circle. The sudden movement to port throws the Joker and his men to the deck, flat on their backs, and the bags of poison slide to the middle away from the railing. Batman runs back on deck and tosses the thugs one by one overboard, and then radios to a police launch to fish them out. "Any more tricks up your sleeve?" asks Batman, turning to face the Joker. "It's just you and me, now. Want to try and see which of us can punch harder?" Batman makes a fist. "I guess I know a punchline when I hear one," concedes the Clown Prince, holding out his wrists for the Bat-Cuffs. "I give up."

The End

As the Batmobile approaches the Gotham Suburban Airport entrance, Batman sees this note taped to the gatehouse door: "Time is running out! In a few short hours, we will completely terrorize Gotham City! Ha ha ha!" Batman reads the note carefully. *This is the Joker's handiwork,* he thinks grimly. *Could there be a clue within it? Or is it a red herring? I can't spend too long puzzling over it. As the Joker says, time is running out!*

If Batman runs onto the airfield, turn to page 12.

If he takes the time to puzzle out the note, turn to page 18.

The driver is a teenager who explains that a mysterious stranger gave him ten dollars to drive this "fake" Batmobile away as a joke. "You've been the victim of a hoax," says Batman, motioning the lad out and sliding behind the wheel. Leaving the bewildered teen far behind, Batman speeds off. *There's only one person who would dupe that kid and try to poison me—all as a joke,* he thinks grimly. *That Crafty Contriver of Crimes must be out of jail again—the JOKER!* Suddenly, Batman sees a large red sign in the road ahead. It reads: DETOUR: CONSTRUCTION. *Strange,* thinks Batman. *This road shouldn't be under construction . . .*

If Batman takes the detour, turn to page 2.

If he gets out to investigate, turn to page 31.

For further information on the Joker, turn to page 118.

Batman quickly unfolds a compact face mask from his utility belt and attaches it to an emergency oxygen tank. Then he breaks a small smoke bomb capsule, and rolls away from the rag pile. As the choking Joker frantically tries to stamp out the trick "fire," Batman summons the police on his two-way radio. Later, after the Joker is captured, an officer restores Batman to normal size by throwing the helmet's switch to ENLARGE. "It takes a big man to admit it when he needs help, Batman," says the officer "Right you are!" laughs Batman, leaping into the Batmobile. "But until you showed up, I was only two inches tall!"

The End

"That was YOUR skull on the Bat-Signal," chuckles the Terrible Trickster, "and it was YOUR doom I predicted in the newspaper. Ha ha ha!" He reaches for the valve on the gas tank. But Batman has decided it is time to act. He swiftly dons a gas mask and releases a potent sleeping gas from a tiny Bat-Canister on his utility belt. "Pleasant dreams, Joker," says Batman on his way out the door. "It looks like this time you've been out-GASSED by Batman!"

The End

There is a bright flash of light and a loud piercing noise, and suddenly Batman is only two inches tall! "Isn't this a GREAT practical joke??!!" booms the Barnum of Buffoonery. "I've outwitted you with *wit!* Ha ha!" Suddenly, he opens a cloth sack, and out springs a common housecat. And Batman is the exact size of a mouse! "Oops!" chuckles the Joker, "I'm afraid I've let the cat out of the bag! Ha ha!"

If Batman tries to outrun the cat, turn to page 46.

If he crawls under the metal helmet on the floor, turn to page 30.

Batman runs to a crop-dusting plane on the airfield. *Hmmm*, he thinks, inspecting the plane closely. *All fueled up and ready to go . . . and these metal containers are filled with lethal toxins!* He radios Commissioner Gordon to report the plane. "The Joker," says Batman, "plans to 'dust' Gotham City with a chemical poison—and there's enough in these containers to kill half the population . . ." But before he can finish, Batman is dealt a heavy blow to the jaw and his radio smashed. He is surrounded by the Joker's men. It must be six against one!

If Batman keeps fighting, turn to page 34.

If he pretends to be knocked unconscious, turn to page 78.

Batman suddenly kicks out with all his strength, knocking the Joker backward into his gang, who tumble into the cockpit and jam the wheel. He quickly wriggles free of his bonds, but the plane is headed into a nosedive! As the Joker and his thugs take the only parachutes and bail out, Batman tries to free the stuck wheel. But it won't budge! Suddenly, the radio

crackles with a message. "This is the Joker calling Batman from my parachute walkie-talkie! Didn't I give you enough clues, dummy? You fell for every trick and now you're just plain falling! *GET IT?* 'PLANE FALLING'?! Ha ha ha!"

The End

Listening at the locked door of the deserted gasworks plant, Batman hears sounds coming from inside. He climbs silently to the skylight on the roof. In the darkness below, he can see a band of intruders hooking up a large steel tank to the city's main gas pipeline. The deadly toxin! Plunging through the skylight in a shower of broken glass, Batman crashes down hard on the band of thugs. But a familiar voice emerges from the darkness: "Not very clever, Batman! You've walked right into my trap. Heh heh heh!" It's the Joker!

If Batman decides to wait and hear the Joker out, turn to page 10.

If he decides to rush the Prince of Pranksters, turn to page 4.

Batman studies the riddle. "Let's see," he says to himself. "First the Riddler says IF YOU CAN READ—which is what people do with newspapers. Then he says IF YOU CAN WATCH—which is what people do with . . . that's it! Television! The news on television!" Rushing into the nearest department store, Batman asks the manager to turn to the news on one of the store's TV sets. To their astonishment, the Riddler is on the air! He has taken over the television studio! "Hello, Batman!" he shouts into the camera. "I know you solved the first riddle—that was easy! Now try this one: I'LL TAKE A CHANCE: THE PLAY'S THE THING. I'LL MAKE YOU DANCE—A PUPPET ON A STRING!"

If Batman ignores the riddle and rushes to the television studio, turn to page 37.

If he finds a double meaning in the Riddler's message, turn to page 41.

Climbing up on the narrow steel ledge in the phone booth, Batman is momentarily above the gas. "Now," he grunts, "if I can just—punch out this metal panel—at the top—!"

Locking his fingers together on his head to cushion the blow, Batman springs straight up. His muscular body collides like a missile with the top of the phone booth and pops the lid right off! Taking a deep gulp of fresh air, Batman does two complete somersaults and makes a perfect landing in the front seat of the Batmobile, just as it is turning to speed off!

"The *Batman!*" shouts the astonished driver, slamming on the brakes. "You mean this really *is* the Batmobile?!"

Turn to page 8.

"Batman! Thank heavens you're here!" exclaims Commissioner Gordon, as the Caped Crusader arrives at Police Headquarters. "Look at this edition of the Gotham *Gazette!*" The headline reads: 24 HOURS TO DOOM! A WARNING TO BATMAN!

"Can this mean you have twenty-four hours to live?" asks the Commissioner. But Batman is studying the headline. "It takes a clever mind to sneak into the Gotham Printers and add this headline. This is the Joker's work!" But it is almost dawn, and today is the day Bruce Wayne is to go on a charity cruise. Should Batman ignore the warning and go on the cruise as Bruce, or should he investigate the Gotham *Gazette* while the trail's still hot?

If Batman goes on the cruise as planned, turn to page 40.

If he rushes over to the newspaper office, turn to page 5.

Batman stands puzzling over the enigmatic note, when he is suddenly surrounded by gunmen, all laughing and pointing pistols at him. Out strides the Joker, laughing loudest of all. "Ha ha! Oh, this is so much fun," he cackles, forcing Batman across the airfield to the hangar. "Welcome to your own execution!" laughs the Joker. He points to a noosed rope tied to the rafters overhead. "You get your choice between hanging in the hangar or"—he points to a metal chair with wires attached to it—"or being electrocuted! Ha ha! Decide NOW, or I'll have you shot!"

If Batman chooses hanging, turn to page 59.

If he chooses "the chair," turn to page 36.

"The last piece of the puzzle!" exclaims Batman, as the President's aides scramble for candles. "BLIND AS A BAT must mean the Riddler has disrupted the city's power supply and cut the electricity! FOUNDING FATHERS must refer to Washington itself! And BREAK FLAT must be another way of saying 'to make flat broke'—the Riddler is planning a big heist!" The question is, where?

If he intercepts the Riddler at the U.S. Mint, turn to page 84.

If he flies in Air Force One to try to stop the biggest heist in history, turn to page 90.

Just as the Joker and his men are about to pour the chemical poison, Batman yanks the Batarang from his utility belt and hurls it. The tiny device circles noiselessly, spinning a silken cord, around and around the gang. Suddenly, Batman pulls tight on the cord and binds the Joker and his gang together. They are completely helpless!

Batman radios Commissioner Gordon and tells him of the Joker's mad plot. "I know you'd like to talk to him, Commissioner," says Batman into his two-way radio, "but he's all tied up at the moment!" The Joker doesn't seem to get the joke. He just stares straight ahead, frowning, as Batman steers for shore.

The End

As he is being swung around, Batman has spied a pile of old rags in one corner of the shed. With a perfect estimate of his trajectory, he unfastens his cape, sails free into the air, executes a precise somersault, and dives safely into the pile of rags. They break his fall like a dozen soft mattresses.

The trouble is the rags are soaked with turpentine! COUGH! COUGH! *If I don't think fast*, chokes Batman, *I'll suffocate!*

If Batman struggles down to the bottom of the rag pile, turn to page 39.

If he uses his utility belt, turn to page 9.

Batman opens the door, and with a THUD he is knocked unconscious! When he comes to, his hands and feet are bound, and the Joker is standing over him. He holds a strange-looking metal helmet with a switch on either side. One side reads ENLARGE, and the other REDUCE. "Just a little gadget I stole from the Gotham Institute of Technology," laughs the Joker. "Ooooh! I'm about to reach the zenith of zaniness! Ha ha ha! How would you like to SHRINK, Batman? Hee hee!" As Batman struggles to break free, the Joker places the helmet on his head and throws the REDUCE switch.

Turn to page 11.

Batman is suddenly seized by the Riddler's men and tied up! They all wear odd-looking eyeglasses. "These special INFRARED glasses," sneers the Riddler, "should give you a hint why I caused the blackout. Not that it matters, since this is where you make your exit, Batman!" The Riddler turns on a giant turbine, and shoves Batman down into the machinery, between the sharp blades of a giant wheel and a pounding steel piston!

If Batman twists toward the piston, turn to page 71.

If he twists toward the wheel, turn to page 35.

With a mighty thrust and a last gasp, Batman kicks the door with both feet. But it is made of doubly reinforced steel and bulletproof glass. It doesn't budge.

"Ha ha!" comes a maniacal laugh from the dangling telephone receiver. "You should have guessed what the grinning skull meant, Batman! I've outwitted you at last!" Which of Batman's foes has beaten him? He thinks he recognizes the laugh, but he is losing consciousness. He'll never know!

"At last!" continues the crazy voice, "the last laugh at last! Ha ha ha! Have you guessed who this is, yet? Well, I'll tell you! I am—"

But Batman can hear no longer.

The End

"Since we don't trust each other, Riddler . . ." says Batman slowly, "why don't we compromise? Let's have this movie company *film* my unmasking right now?" The Riddler loves the idea. "Perfect!" he says. "It's so much more dramatic!" Batman calls the movie director over and whispers to him. The director shouts to the Riddler: "Turn the crane around! Your left profile is better than your right." The appeal to his vanity works, and for a split second the Riddler is turned away. Batman swings into the cab of the crane feet first, knocking the Riddler twenty feet away, right into the arms of the security guards. Then he gently lowers the actor, unhurt, to the ground.

As the Riddler is hauled off to jail, Batman calls after him, "Don't forget when they take your mug shots, your left profile's better!" But the only thing the Riddler can think of in clever reply is "Bah!"

The End

Commissioner Gordon's deep voice comes crackling over the Batmobile's radio. "Yes, we know about the Bat-Signal," he says. "My men are working on repairing it right now. But there's more urgent business—you are scheduled to be in Washington, D.C., tomorrow for the July 4th celebration! You'd better get started right away—your country calls!"

If Batman is suspicious and goes to talk in person with the Commissioner, turn to page 63.

If he takes the Batplane to Washington, turn to page 49.

Batman leaps to one side as the mammoth coin rumbles out the front entrance. "Look out!" calls Batman to the pedestrians in the street. "Run for your lives!" In the meantime, the Riddler and his men escape! Batman rushes around to the back alley in time to see the getaway car pulling away. Just then, the huge coin, having first rolled up the street, now rolls back down it, plowing right into the getaway car and sending the Riddler and his gang sprawling all over the pavement along with their stolen coins and bullion. "With all your cleverness," says Batman, "you shouldn't have relied on the flip of a coin!"

The End

All four villains rush up the tower to the lookout atop the "iceberg" fortress, as Batman and the hostages escape in the confusion. "Look!" gasps the Riddler, pointing ahead. "We're on a collision course!" Terrified, the Joker stutters: "Th-that's not the North Pole! It's the sheer rock-cliffs of Antarctica!" Catwoman hisses: "Batman sabotaged the controls!" But the Scarecrow points down. "Look!" he cries. "They're getting away in our whale-sub!"

Around the world, seismic instruments record the demise of four criminals as the fortress slams into the cliffs. The Doomsday Prophecy has come true—but for the forces of Evil, not Good!

The End

Batman strains against his rope bonds, breaking them. He reaches into his utility belt, and sets off a small flash bomb. The sudden light blinds the Joker and his henchmen. As they rub their eyes and stagger about the plane in confusion, it doesn't take the Caped Crusader long to subdue the crooks and secure them with his Bat-Rope. He disconnects the switch on the poison spray nozzle, rendering it useless. As he takes control of the plane, Batman tells the Joker, "I'm changing your course! We're flying nonstop to the Gotham Police Airfield!"

The End

"Not too clever, Batman!" roars the Joker as Batman races over and slips under the brim of the metal helmet. "That won't get you anywhere!" The Joker picks up the helmet, but to his amazement Batman has completely disappeared! Suddenly, he hears a small voice that seems to come out of thin air: "Even you can reach me no longer, Joker! The helmet has made me too small for the eye to see!" But the Merry Master of Mayhem refuses to be thwarted. "Oh, no, you don't, Batman!" he shouts, throwing the reduction switch into reverse, "I'll just return you to a manageable little mouse size . . ."

Turn to page 48.

Batman leaves the Batmobile to investigate. On the door of the construction shed is a stenciled sign: GOTHAM DESTRUCTION COMPANY. *That should read CON-struction*, thinks Batman with a frown. *These are pretty grim jokes— first a skull on the Bat-Signal and now this sign. They add up to DEATH and DESTRUC-TION!*

Should Batman take this warning seriously and return to the Batmobile? Or should he call the Joker's bluff, and go into the shed?

If Batman goes back to the Bat-mobile and continues on the detour road, turn to page 2.

If he enters the shed, turn to page 22.

Batman tosses his Flash-Batarang, temporarily blinding the giant Joker who lets go of him in midswing! "Batman has vanished!" shouts the Joker to his gang as he opens the door. "Find him!" They report back that they saw nothing except a real bat hanging upside down from a rafter. "You fools!" screams the Machiavelli of Mischief, climbing the ladder. "Bats don't sleep at night! They're nocturnal!" But Batman has already escaped through a tiny hole in the roof, locked the Joker and his gang in the shed, and run off to the Gotham Institute, where experts will help him regain his normal size.

"Outwitted by a brain the size of a bat's!" moans the Joker as tears of frustration stream down his face.

The End

"*Something* strange is going on," says Batman, parking the Batmobile near the huge reservoir. Far out in the middle of the water is a ferryboat! He runs and jumps into a small power launch belonging to the Department of Public Works. "Pleasure boating on the reservoir is illegal!" he says to himself. Shutting off his motor to approach the ferry undetected, Batman now sees the Joker's gang aboard the larger boat. They are opening bags of some kind of dry chemical to dump overboard. Commanding his crooked crew is the Joker, who laughs hysterically. Batman listens to their conversation.

Turn to page 56.

Just as Batman starts knocking heads together, there is a hard THWACK as he is struck on the back of his head!

When he regains consciousness, Batman is bound and gagged and lying on the floor of the plane. It has taken off! The Joker and his men are all there. "As Gotham City wakes up today," gloats the Joker, taking hold of the switch on the spray nozzle connected to the toxins, "we'll just swoop down and lightly dust them with poison!"

If Batman lashes out with his feet, turn to page 13.

If he uses his utility belt, turn to page 29.

Batman grabs the wheel's hub as he falls, spins around with it, and collides with the Riddler's chest. He knocks off the gang's infrared glasses with one deft toss of his Batarang. As they stumble around in the dark, Batman puts on the Riddler's glasses. "Now who's blind as a bat?" he asks, tying up the gang for the police. "It looks like you'll be hogging the headlines on Independence Day, Riddler. I can see the papers now: RIDDLER BEHIND BARS FOR LIFE!"

The End

Seeing that he's outnumbered, Batman decides to go limp and let himself be strongarmed over to the chair. But he has noticed that the chair is wired to the airport hangar's main power source. "Don't I get a last request?" asks Batman sadly. "Oh, goody!" giggles the Monarch of Mirth. "Of course you do! But no tricks, now!" Batman asks to say a short prayer and then kneels with his back to the Joker and his gang. Quickly, Batman switches the wires connected to the chair and then turns around. The Joker straps him in and throws the main switch. With a loud POP! everything goes dark. Batman has caused a short circuit. In the dark, Batman clobbers the gang. He even wipes the smile off the Joker's face!

The End

If I'm fast enough, thinks Batman, hurrying across town, *I'll get to the studio before the Riddler leaves the air!* Running into the control room, Batman sees the Riddler's face still on all the monitors, saying, ". . . So, good luck, Batman! May the cleverest man win!" But when Batman enters the studio, it's empty and all the cameras are turned off! Too late, Batman has realized his mistake. The Riddler was never here—he was only a prerecorded tape!

What's worse, the Evening News on another station announces that the Riddler has outwitted Batman, and that his men have been busy robbing every bank in Washington—while Batman went on a wild goose chase!

The End

Batman pulls a grappling hook from his utility belt, and throws it at a low aluminum table in the waiting area, pulling it quickly into the path of the twelve-foot coin. Inches before it can crush Batman, the coin hits the table, tilting its disc top and pivoting on a ninety-degree angle away from Batman. It rumbles right smack into the wall in front of the Riddler and his escaping gang!

Later, after Batman and the police have captured the crooks, Batman examines the stolen trays, bags, and cases. "U.S. Mint coin-stamping plates!" he explains. "So that was your plan, Riddler: to glut the market with counterfeit coins and destroy the economy!" He turns with a smile and points at the huge metal statue embedded in the wall. "Well, it looks like another counterfeit coin stopped you!"

The End

Batman works his way down through the rags to the floor of the shed, which is made of wooden planks. He drops through a knothole to the world outside, and comes face to face with the cat! The last thing Batman sees before the huge beast pounces, is the giant eye of the Joker peering through the knothole in the floor above. "What a way to go, eh, Batman? To end up as just an insignificant bit of . . . BATnip! Tsk, tsk! Ha ha ha!"

The End

Batman arrives the next day at Gotham Harbor in the guise of his secret identity, Bruce Wayne, millionaire playboy. He and his fellow passengers—among the richest people in the U.S.—have donated thousands to charity by joining this cruise. Everyone seems in good spirits, but Bruce is secretly worried about the strange Bat-Signal warning. What if some criminal mastermind has deduced that Batman is in reality a rich man—a wealthy citizen of Gotham? Bruce hesitates on the gangplank. Could this charity cruise be a trap?

If Bruce boards the yacht, turn to page 94.

If he stays on shore, turn to page 51.

Hmmm, thinks Batman, considering the riddle. *THE PLAY'S THE THING is just an expression, but I wonder . . .* He opens to the entertainment section of the newspaper he bought. There is an ad for a children's show called "The Riddle," and an article about a movie company that starts shooting a new Batman movie at the Washington Monument today. "I don't have any time to lose!" says Batman. "I know the way the Riddler works! If I don't act fast, he'll pull some evil stunt!"

If Batman goes to the movie shoot, turn to page 54.

If he rushes to the children's theater, turn to page 89.

From his utility belt, Bruce secretly removes a sonar scrambling device and slips it in his ear. It prevents him from being affected as Mesmor hypnotizes the audience. "Batman," Mesmor whispers to the hypnotized millionaires, "you are listening to the voice of Two-Face! You will do as I say, and reveal your secret identity." But the audience is silent. "Good!" says Two-Face under his disguise as Mesmor. "Batman isn't on this cruise, or he would have revealed himself. . . . Now, everybody hand over his money!" But before the crook can escape with his loot by stepping into a getaway speedboat, Batman collars him. "You were wrong, Two-Face," he says. "I *did* come along on this cruise. But YOU are definitely NOT my favorite charity!"

The End

Quickly estimating the distance between him and the deadly weapon, Batman lunges at the flamethrower before the henchman can pull the trigger. Twisting the mechanism free and throwing it into the water, Batman turns around, firmly gripping the dazed henchman. But Two-Face has disappeared!

"Batman!" shouts a handsome man in the crowd. "He went that way! I'll tie up that crook and hold him for the police, if you'll follow Two-Face!"

If Batman takes the stranger's suggestion, turn to page 77.

If he smells a rat, turn to page 83.

It is a monstrous creature, bigger than an ocean liner, plowing through the waves! So as not to reveal his secret identity, Bruce helps herd everyone below decks. As soon as the last man jumps below, the whale rams the ship! There is a catastrophic smashing sound as the ship splinters in two. Hundreds of tons of salt water pour in over everyone.

The last thought Bruce Wayne has before going down for the third time is: "What good did it do to save Batman's secret identity?"

The End

Batman races for the open door, stops short, and ducks. The surprised cat leaps right over him and out the door. Batman spins around and shoves the door with all his might, slamming it shut. "Very good, little Batman," laughs the Joker in delight. "I like you this size! You're a lot more fun!" The Joker reaches down so suddenly that Batman doesn't have time to dodge. He grabs Batman's cape and swings the tiny crimefighter around his head. "I hope you can fly, like the other little bats! Ha ha!"

If Batman unfastens his cape, turn to page 21.

If he uses one of the Batarangs in his utility belt, turn to page 32.

For further information on the utility belt, turn to page 119.

But to the Joker's shock, the full-sized Batman suddenly appears, knocking him flat with a sock to the jaw. "I'm afraid you weren't as clever as you thought, Joker," says Batman, slapping cuffs on the Cowed Clown. "You see, when you picked up the helmet, I was clinging to the inside and pretending to have shrunk to invisibility so you would reverse the switch and return me to normal size. Why aren't you laughing? *I* thought it was a pretty good joke. And by the way," he adds, hauling the Joker out the door and glancing at the cat, "you two should really pick on someone your own size!"

The End

Much later in Washington, the first thing Batman sees is a newsstand, with the headlines screaming: RIDDLER PROCLAIMS END OF BATMAN! SAYS: "IF YOU CAN READ, THIS NEWS IS NEW. IF YOU CAN WATCH, THE REST YOU'LL VIEW!" A threat and a riddle from one of Batman's worst enemies! "Hmmm," says Batman. "If I know the Riddler, he means business . . . and he won't let anyone—even the President of the United States—stand in his way!"

If Batman tries to solve the riddle, turn to page 15.

If he hurries to the White House, turn to page 57.

For further information on the Riddler, turn to page 118.

Batman boldly swings down into the mouth of the leviathan, clearing its sharp, conical teeth and landing almost as far in as its gullet. There, waist deep in water, are the twelve terrified millionaires—still alive! "Hold onto the lower teeth!" shouts Batman, as the huge beast turns again toward the cruise ship. "It looks like he's going to swallow the rest of the passengers. All the water pouring in will wash us into the whale's stomach if we don't hold on!"

If Batman also holds on, turn to page 100.

If he keeps his hands free to help catch the new victims, turn to page 72.

Bruce remains on shore as the cruise boat sails, keeping a sharp eye out for criminal types, recording faces with his photographic memory. Nearby, a newsman is talking into a remote video camera: "Only one of the millionaires has decided to remain on land. It may have dawned on Mr. Bruce Wayne that some criminal mastermind is planning to expose Batman's secret identity and destroy him. Since he was the only millionaire smart enough to deduce this—he must be BATMAN!" Suddenly, the cameraman turns, revealing the camera to be a mini-blowtorch aimed right at Bruce Wayne! The "newsman" turns to show Bruce the other side of his face—revealing the ugly, scarred visage of the notorious Two-Face!

If Bruce, as Batman, goes into action to protect the crowd, turn to page 117.

If he flings himself into the harbor, turn to page 80.

For more information on Two-Face, turn to page 118.

Gripping the wheel of the jeep, Batman drives straight toward the tank! He veers in front of it, chucking a tear-gas canister from his utility belt, into the hatch. Within seconds, the Riddler and his men come choking out of the tank, tears streaming down their faces.

Later, the gold bullion restored to Fort Knox, Batman explains to the President's chief aide: "When the Riddler proclaimed the END OF BATMAN, he meant the end of my career if I couldn't prevent this robbery . . . but now, the Riddler is doing crossword puzzles in jail!"

The End

Inside the pilot house, Bruce discovers that someone has knocked the helmsman unconscious and wrenched the ship's wheel. *Got to protect Batman's secret identity*, thinks Bruce, as the crew saves the drenched millionaires. *But it's beginning to look like someone wants me to tip my hand.*

Later that night, all the guests on board are invited to be entertained by MESMOR THE MAGNIFICENT, a performer whose gimmick is harmless hypnotism. When Mesmor, a tall handsome man with a waxy complexion, enters the room, Bruce becomes suspicious. He looks vaguely familiar. While Mesmor places the audience under hypnosis, Bruce thinks, *Where have I seen him before?*

If Bruce reaches into his concealed utility belt, turn to page 42.

If he sneaks out of the auditorium, turn to page 75.

Later, at the Washington Monument, an actor playing Batman wears a harness under his costume, to which wires are attached. He is hauled 150 feet up in the air, by means of a giant crane, so it will appear he is climbing the monument with the agility of the real Batman. Suddenly, the crane operator jerks the wires up and down, making the actor-Batman dance—"like a puppet on a string!" It's the Riddler, disguised as a crane operator! He shouts, "If you want to save this actor's life, Batman, unmask yourself and reveal your true identity—or I'll release the wire!"

If Batman runs toward the crane, turn to page 81.

If he agrees to the Riddler's demand, turn to page 58.

Climbing into the crane cab from above is Batman! "B-but wh-where did *you* come from?" stammers the Riddler, as Batman arrests him and puts handcuffs on his wrists. "I just switched places with the actor's *stunt double!* He was standing by ready to do the dangerous acrobatic stunts required for the film. That's who all America saw take off his mask! And once the authorities have you under guard, I'll be able to rescue the actor from the crane! Nice try, Riddler, but as usual, I'm one step ahead of you!"

The End

"How long will it take for this poison to work, Boss?" one of the gang asks the Joker. "I told you, idiot!" he screams. "From the moment we pour it into the reservoir until the time it reaches every home in Gotham takes about twenty hours. At least half the population of Gotham will drink it. The poison will only be active in their systems for a few minutes, but by that time, I'll have won! Batman wasn't clever enough to thwart my scheme!" laughs the Joker. He goes to the starboard railing to dump the first bag of poison. Batman has to act fast!

If Batman reaches for his utility belt, turn to page 20.

If he rushes into the boat's cabin, turn to page 6.

For further information about Batman's utility belt, turn to page 119.

When Batman arrives, the President's chief aide hands him a second riddle delivered only moments before. Batman reads it carefully:

I'LL BREAK THE FOUNDING
    FATHERS FLAT
WHEN EVERYONE'S BLIND AS A BAT.

"What's the Riddler up to?" says the aide. "First he seems to threaten you, then *this*—a riddle that *makes no sense!*"

Suddenly, all the lights go out! Batman rushes to the window in time to see lights winking out all over the city. A power blackout in the nation's capital could be disastrous! Batman must do something!

If Batman rushes to the city's main powerhouse, turn to page 88.

If he has already solved the mysterious riddles, turn to page 19.

"Wait!" shouts Batman, stopping still. "I'll agree to reveal my secret identity, if it will save that actor's life!" Batman reaches up to remove his cowl. "Oh, no, you don't!" shouts the Riddler. "You just trot right over to the television studio. You're going to reveal your identity on live television for the whole world to see! And *that* is what I meant by the END OF BATMAN!" Everyone on the film crew watches helplessly. The poor figure high up in the air dangles uncertainly, and the Riddler reaches for the wire release control, as Batman decides what to do next.

If Batman agrees to go to the studio, turn to page 91.

If he suggests bringing a television crew on location, turn to page 25.

Batman gives up and walks over to the noose, which the Joker happily places around the Caped Crusader's neck. But he has forgotten about Batman's acrobatic ability. As the men pull on the rope, Batman grabs hold of it and kicks out, sending his body around in a wide arc and slipping his head out of the noose at the same time! Before the gang can get off a single shot, Batman knocks their heads together and wraps the unconscious thugs in the hanging rope with the Joker in the middle!

"Until I can get the police," says Batman, walking out and locking the door, "this hangar will make a perfect holding cell! Nighty-night, boys!"

The End

"I'm not letting them get away!" says Batman, picking up speed. The Bat-Sub keeps up with the whale-sub far north into the North Atlantic. *That's a* very *big iceberg!* thinks Batman. The shape on his radar screen shows an iceberg many hundreds of feet high, and nearly a quarter-mile wide. And the whale-sub is headed straight for it! "I don't get it," says Batman. "They're on a suicide course!" Suddenly, the whale-sub disappears from the radar screen. Did it collide with the iceberg?

If Batman surfaces, turn to page 101.

If he aims the Bat-Sub for the iceberg, turn to page 93.

Thank goodness I finished testing this device last week, thinks Batman, removing his new Sprinkler-Batarang from his utility belt. He flings it out over the theater, where it releases a shower of chemical fire extinguisher. The flames are out, and the children are safe. In seconds, Batman has opened a trapdoor to the roof, letting in fresh air. In the street below he spots the Riddler, dressed in black, escaping with his Batman puppet. With another skillful throw, Batman hooks him by a Bat–Grappling Hook and hauls him up, dangling from the roof. After alerting the police on his two-way radio, Batman calls down to the Riddler, "Now who's a puppet on a string?" But the Riddler is out of riddles.

The End

There was something odd about the Commissioner's voice, thinks Batman after shutting off the radio. *It sounded somehow . . . mechanical!* Within minutes, Batman arrives at the Commissioner's office to find a very upset Sergeant Bullock. "The Commissioner's been kidnapped!" he cries. "And we have no clues!" But Batman examines an electric clock on the floor. It broke when it fell, and the time recorded is five minutes before Batman spoke to the Commissioner by radio! *Gordon must have knocked this over*, thinks Batman, *to warn me the voice wasn't his!*

If Batman checks out the police switchboard, turn to page 105.

If he rushes to the Gotham Transmission Tower, turn to page 68.

Batman swings back on deck, and has all the millionaires grab long-handled shuffleboard cues and stand ready. When the whale lunges open-mouthed at them, Batman gives the signal. "Now!" he cries, and they all ram their cues into the monster's jaws, jamming his mouth open. Out tumble the dozen passengers who were trapped in his maw! Confused, the angry monster plunges to the bottom of the sea.

Later, having returned to his secret identity as Bruce Wayne, with no one the wiser, Batman thinks: *The FEED THE HUNGRY Charity Cruise almost meant FEED THE FISH!*

The End

"You may have the upper hand," says Batman to the crooked conglomerate, "and your cleverly disguised submarine may be a powerful vessel, but your electrical system is crude!" With that, he whips a Razor-Batarang at the electrical wires leading to the fluorescent light in the ceiling. In a flash of sparks, the Batarang severs the wires and plunges the sub into darkness. Then Batman leaps from one villain to the next, finding them in the dark with a tiny radar device. In minutes he has bound and gagged the criminals and left them behind. A quick inspection of the control room shows him how the sub operates. By the end of the day, a giant, whale-shaped submarine has sailed into Gotham Harbor, depositing not only many of America's most prominent citizens, but also four of its worst public enemies!

The End

"I'll admit defeat, Two-Face," says Batman, "if you'll let these innocent people go!" He secretly works loose the lining of his cape. Two-Face only laughs. "I want revenge on all the world, Batman! Not just you! But before they get theirs, I'm going to make you look like me . . ." At this, he grabs the flamethrower from his henchman. "Let me!" he shouts, pulling the trigger. But Batman has removed the asbestos lining of his cape and thrown it over his head. It protects him from the flames. He dives forward, sending both men into Gotham Harbor, where a police boat picks them up. When the crowd looks around, Batman has vanished. A few minutes later, another police launch saves Bruce Wayne from the water.

The End

Batman arrives at the tall Gotham Transmission Tower. Silhouetted against the night sky, the tower and all the crisscrossing high tension wires present an ominous sight. Suddenly, a ghostly voice seems to come from atop the tower: "Batman! Help! It's me, the Commissioner!" Batman looks around quickly. He also hears macabre laughter, echoing loudly from a nearby amusement park. *That sounds far too loud to be natural*, thinks Batman. *Could it be another clue?* But the voice from above beckons, "Help me! He'll kill me!"

If Batman climbs the tower, turn to page 115.

If Batman investigates the amusement park, turn to page 113.

Batman turns unthinkingly down a narrow passageway. "Ha ha!" laughs the Joker as Batman slips on the slick surface of the acrylic corridor. He is completely surrounded by pure, clear acrylic! Through the stuff he can see the four villains laughing at him, but he can't break through the hard walls to grab them. "We knew you were here all along," screams the Joker. "We decided to trap you like this for—well, for the FUN of it!" shouts the Riddler. The Scarecrow and Catwoman laugh so hard they can't talk.

Batman is trapped inside a war machine of enemies of the U.S.—and he's powerless against his archfoes!

The End

"Quick, kids!" shouts Batman, raising the asbestos curtain, so the audience can climb backstage. After they are all safely out of the theater, he drops the curtain, confining the flames. "Everybody into the fresh air!" he says, leading them out the back door. *The Riddler made me dance like a puppet on a string,* thinks Batman angrily. *I had to let him escape, but it was more important to save the lives of these children. Someday I'll meet him again!*

The End

The Riddler and his men watch triumphantly as Batman falls into the machinery. After shutting off the power, the Riddler removes a torn Bat-Cape. "This is all that's left of his pulverized costume, men!"

Later, as the gang robs the darkened Treasury Building, making the "Founding Fathers" flat broke while "everyone is blind as a bat," Batman turns on the lights and arrests them all. "I timed the intervals of the pounding steel piston," says Batman, "slipping through, hiding behind the machinery and removing my cape. I followed you here with my tiny infrared flashlight. Now here's a riddle for *you:* 'What goes to jail and never gets out?'"

The End

Batman selflessly disregards his own safety, and catches one millionaire after another as they are swept into the open mouth of the whale. He helps each person grip a separate tooth, but suddenly a powerful wave of sea water catches him off guard, the monster swallows, and Batman is washed down the giant, dark throat, plunging deep into the belly of the beast!

Turn to page 95.

Resetting the controls, Batman runs off in the direction of the gunshots. Ahead he finds one of the millionaires, his arm wounded. "The Riddler!" he gasps to Batman. "He's got a gun!" But Batman is not afraid of the Riddler's gun. It's the noise it makes that worries him.

After giving the man first aid, Batman runs into a darker passageway in the acrylic walls. He must save the lives of these wealthy citizens, but it's also his duty to stop his four archenemies! He hears another gunshot, and makes his decision.

If Batman calls out to the millionaires to head for the whale-sub, turn to page 108.

If he pretends to give himself up, turn to page 92.

Hovering just outside the underwater cave entrance, Batman floods the inside with light. There's nothing there! It's just an empty cave! "Got the drop on you, Batman!" comes a booming voice from above, over a sonar loudspeaker. He turns the Bat-Sub for a look and sees the nuclear whale-sub directly above him on the surface, dropping depth charges. They begin exploding all around him. "One of these is going to be a direct hit sooner or later, Batman!" jeers Scarecrow's voice from above. "Yeah!" shouts the Joker, "we could have told you this trip would be a blast!"

If Batman reaches for a specially installed device, turn to page 82.

If he tries to outrun the depth charges, turn to page 114.

Bruce sneaks around to the stage door, where he listens to the show Mesmor is putting on.

Much later, at dinner, as the captain toasts all the philanthropists on board, Bruce stands up, glassy-eyed, and announces that he is Batman! "Aha!" shouts Mesmor from the back, removing the waxy mask that covers his scars. "I, Two-Face, planted a posthypnotic suggestion during my performance. I instructed Batman to reveal his secret identity when the captain gave his customary toast!" But to his surprise, suddenly everyone stands up, glassy-eyed, each one announcing that HE is Batman!

Turn to page 99.

For more information on Two-Face, turn to page 118.

"This time they mean to destroy me!" says Batman to himself. "I'd better try to out-maneuver them!" Luckily, his radar screen is still operational. In it, he can see the faster whale-sub gaining on him. He turns the Bat-Sub around and dives sharply down. It follows. He zooms quickly toward the surface. It follows. Another explosion right behind him breaks a seam, and sea water begins to leak into the Bat-Sub!

If Batman abandons ship, turn to page 109.

If he turns the Bat-Sub around and steers for the open "mouth" of the "whale," turn to page 98.

Leaving the dazed crook in the hands of the handsome stranger, Batman rushes off around the corner in pursuit of Two-Face, but the roads leading away on either side are empty. He searches for a while. Then, he realizes he's been tricked! He runs back to the dock, only to find all the bystanders bound and gagged, and the handsome stranger gone. After Batman removes the gag from one man's mouth, he explains that Batman only saw one side of the handsome stranger's face. *Oh, no!* thinks Batman, ruefully. *I've exposed these innocent people to danger, and let that crook escape!*

The End

"Ooomph!" grunts Batman, falling heavily to the ground as though unconscious. "Perfect!" chortles the Joker to his gang. "The police will be looking for a crop-dusting plane, but we'll use the Gotham Rubber Company blimp, flying over this morning's Independence Day parade. We'll poison the parade-goers! Ha ha!"

But later that morning at the parade, thousands look up to see the Joker and his men slowly lowered to earth in handcuffs! "Citizens of Gotham!" Batman's voice booms out of a loudspeaker. "I'm delivering these crooks to you as symbols of your new INDEPENDENCE from the tyranny of crime! Welcome the Joker with a great big—LAUGH! HA HA!" And the crowd roars!

The End

Turning his jeep around at high speed, Batman zooms to the Air Force Military Police Headquarters, explaining to the officer in charge that this is military business. Soon, Batman is high in the air with a small police force inside a reconnaissance plane, guiding the way to the winding chain of armored trucks below. He points out that the tank leading them is driving to a concealed entrance in the side of a mountain!

Later, during the big July 4th celebration, after electrical power has been restored to Washington, Batman plays a videotape. "These shots were taken today from the air over Kentucky, showing the capture of the Riddler and his gang by combined air and ground forces!" The crowd cheers as the fireworks go off.

The End

Bruce jumps over the side of the pier, just as Two-Face's henchman turns on the flame-thrower. In moments, safely beneath the surface of the water, Bruce Wayne changes into Batman. But when he pulls himself back up onto the pier, he finds all the innocent by-standers lined up against a wall. Two-Face and his henchman train the flamethrower on them. "Well, Batman!" cries Two-Face, the ugly side of his face twisted into an evil grin. "Now everybody knows your secret identity! Announce your retirement, or these people burn to a crisp!"

If Batman rushes them, turn to page 43.

If he tries to reason with the insane criminal, turn to page 67.

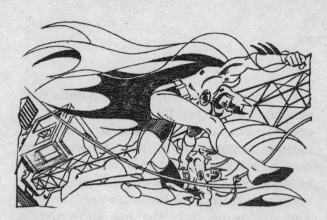

As Batman runs toward the crane, he quickly takes a Bat-Rope from his utility belt. With it, he throws a grappling hook to the top of the tower. Then he swings up, snatching the actor and depositing him safely on the ground, before the Riddler can release the wires. The film crew gasps at this daring rescue. In a flash, Batman leaps into the cab of the crane, grabs the Riddler, and binds him hand and foot.

With the Pathetic Puzzler on his way to jail, the movie director moans, "How will I end my movie?" Batman smiles. "Any ending's okay with me," he says, "just as long as it isn't what it almost was: THE END OF BATMAN!"

The End

I've got one chance left! thinks Batman desperately. He reaches for a red switch on his control panel, labeled VERTICAL MINI-TORPEDO LAUNCH SYSTEM. *This is a one-time-only long shot,* he thinks, taking careful aim through his observation hose, *so it had better be a bull's-eye! I've got to disable the whale-sub!* It works! The explosion seals the big sub's depth-charger, and cripples its engines.

Later, merchant marine ships on the high seas are startled to see a small Bat-Sub towing what looks like a huge wounded whale through the ocean back to the U.S.!

The End

"No, you don't, Two-Face!" shouts Batman, flinging the dazed henchman at the handsome stranger. The two men go sprawling on the ground in front of the crowd. The handsome stranger has landed awkwardly, revealing the ugly side of his face! "A daring and bold move, Two-Face," says Batman, tying them both up. "But you forget I have a photographic memory. I knew that if you had been in the crowd earlier, I would have remembered your face. But since I didn't, you had to be the newsman who had his back to me! Sorry your plot to destroy Batman failed . . ." He pushes the two criminals ahead of him toward the Batmobile. "Now I'm afraid both sides of your face will be looking out from behind bars!"

The End

All gold and silver coins—precious metals—are manufactured by the U.S. Bureau of the Mint, reasons Batman, racing across the darkened city. Just inside the main entrance of the Bureau, he sees the Riddler and his gang carrying bags of money, and sneaking past the huge symbol in the main hall—a twelve-foot replica of a silver dollar. "Give yourselves up!" he shouts. But the Riddler and his men dislodge the heavy coin and start it rolling right at Batman!

If Batman dives to avoid being crushed, turn to page 27.

If he tries to use the giant coin against the Riddler, turn to page 38.

The whale is gigantic—four times normal size! Before the gargantuan mammal can crash into the ship, Bruce emerges from a nearby cabin as Batman. He secures his Bat-Rope to the ship's rigging, swings far out over the whale, and comes down hard on its blowhole with the heel of his foot. *That should hurt him*, thinks Batman. *It's a sensitive spot!* But the whale feels nothing! It keeps plowing through the water toward the terrified passengers on the cruise ship. Batman begins punching the whale's blowhole with his fists. "Ouch!" he cries. "My blows don't even dent this whale blubber!" The whale opens its mighty jaws and passes along the ship, swallowing a dozen millionaires!

If Batman swings back onto the ship, turn to page 64.

If he swings down inside the whale's mouth, turn to page 50.

Still laughing behind him, the four fiends seal Batman in the torpedo tube under the "whale's" fin and pull a switch—expelling him like a torpedo at high speed into the ocean. Just ahead of him is the cruise ship. As he slows down, Batman swims for a batlike craft submerged nearby. Before coming on the cruise as Bruce Wayne, Batman suspected foul play, and sent his Bat-Sub to the area on automatic pilot. He climbs aboard and is soon piloting in the direction he last saw the whale-sub heading. Suddenly, a powerful explosion rocks the tiny sub. The whale-sub has torpedoed Batman!

If Batman takes the offensive and chases the whale-sub, turn to page 61.

If Batman tries to outmaneuver the bigger vessel, turn to page 76.

Washington is the center of our government, thinks Batman, racing across town to the building that houses the hydroelectric generators. *I've got to help restore power!* Inside, it is pitch dark. Batman enters cautiously, to within inches of a huge generator. "Strange that the power is shut off," says Batman to himself. "I wish I could see better." He peers at the immense mechanism. Suddenly, a familiar voice from the darkness makes him spin around. "Talk about 'blind as a bat!'" jeers the Riddler.

Turn to page 23.

Batman arrives at the theater to find that the play "The Riddle" is a puppet show. The puppetmaster is dressed in a hooded black costume. He is working a Batman puppet, which suddenly starts dancing grotesquely. "Here's a riddle," it says in a crazy voice. "What kind of a trap gives you a hot foot?" Suddenly, the flameproof fire curtain falls, sealing off the stage from the audience. Flames and smoke fill the small locked theater! The doomed Batman can hear the Riddler outside laughing: "The answer is—a FIRETRAP! Ha ha!"

If Batman raises the curtain, turn to page 70.

If he uses his utility belt, turn to page 62.

Batman gets clearance to fly to Andrews Air Force Base in Air Force One—the President's personal jet! All is confusion at the base, because of the Washington blackout. As he commandeers a jeep, Batman thinks, *The blackout's meant to distract us from the real emergency! It's a BLIND—like in the riddle. The Riddler is about to BREAK THE FOUNDING FATHERS FLAT!* He drives to Fort Knox, America's gold-bullion repository. Suddenly, bursting out of the front entrance, is a line of armored trucks led by a tank!

If Batman drives back to the Air Force Base, turn to page 79.

If he decides to act now and stop this theft, turn to page 52.

After Batman has left for the studio, the film crew sets up a TV monitor so the Riddler can watch Batman's disgrace on national live television. Soon, several grim-faced police officers appear on screen, escorting Batman to the microphone. Batman looks into the camera and intones, "My fellow Americans, I have come before you today to admit defeat! I have been outwitted by the Riddler!" He pulls off his cowl! At the Washington Monument, the Riddler is beside himself with glee. "I did it!" he screams. "I made Batman reveal his true identity!" But he stops laughing once he hears a voice from above say, "Not quite, Riddler!"

Turn to page 55.

Turning a brightly lit corner, Batman finds himself facing the Riddler and his smoking gun. Later, the gloating Scarecrow, Riddler, Catwoman, and Joker have surrounded Batman and the rich hostages, and made them listen to their diabolical plot. After reaching the North Pole, they plan to hide out until they can finish building their incredible nuclear bomb. They will threaten all the nations of the world with it, enslaving everyone to do their bidding! "From the North Pole, we will rule over all!" cheers the Scarecrow. Batman merely smiles. "I think you'll find the North Pole's a long way from here," he says to their surprise.

Turn to page 28.

"Nuclear submarines don't just disappear," says Batman, steering toward the iceberg. He guides his small craft slowly around the outside of the floating mountain of ice deep beneath the surface, scrutinizing his radar screen all the way. Still, no sign of the whale-sub. Turning on his powerful headlights, Batman peers through the porthole. Suddenly, up ahead, carved into the side of the ice, is an enormous underwater cave entrance!

If Batman keeps his distance, but observes the inside by headlights, turn to page 74.

If he throws caution to the winds and enters the cave, turn to page 111.

Soon, the cruise ship is on the high seas, with wealthy millionaires strolling the deck and chatting. Waving in the breeze, a banner reads: FEED THE HUNGRY CHARITY CRUISE. Bruce Wayne discovers he's not the only one to sink a small fortune in this charity. *Hmmm,* he thinks. *All these people are well-known millionaires.* Just then, the entire ship lurches to one side, spilling several millionaires into the sea! *Something must have happened to the helmsman as he was steering this ship,* thinks Bruce. *It could all be an elaborate trick to get Batman to reveal himself. But somebody has to save those men from drowning!*

If Bruce rushes down to the empty lounge on the lower deck, turn to page 102.

If he runs to the pilot house, turn to page 53.

It is pitch dark as Batman lands hard in a pool of water. "Strange!" he says, as he struggles to gain a footing. "This whale's heartbeat sounds . . . mechanical!" Suddenly, the stomach of the whale is flooded with artificial light! There, standing above him on a metal scaffolding, are four of Batman's worst enemies: the Scarecrow, the Joker, the Riddler, and the Catwoman! "Ha ha! This is no whale," laughs the Joker, "it's a nuclear submarine!" The Scarecrow chimes in, "Neatly disguised, eh?" The Riddler points a gun at Batman. "Get in the torpedo tube, fast!" Catwoman adds, "We're sending you back with the good news—tell the U.S. Government in Washington that we are holding the richest men in America hostage. You can just imagine the ransom we're asking!"

If Batman does as they command, turn to page 87.

If he springs into action, turn to page 65.

I'm sure TRUNK CALL is a clue, thinks Batman, throwing open the trunk of the Batmobile. Inside, bound and gagged and squirming frantically, is Commissioner Gordon! Batman removes the gag and starts to untie him. "Batman!" says the terrified Commissioner, "Run! Quick! It's a trap—!" Too late, Batman notices the copper wires leading from the trunk's spring latch to a large bundle of explosives.

Two blocks away, in the dark shadow of an alley, a concealed figure gleefully claps his hands at the sound of a powerful explosion. The Riddler has triumphed!

The End

Batman decides to take the risk and aims the Bat-Sub right into the ice wall next to the embedded whale. But instead of a crash, the ice parts smoothly, and then closes over the front end of the craft, like a living dock. As he steps into the interior of the iceberg, Batman is astonished to find it is not made of ice, but of a superpolymer acrylic substance, harder than diamond, yet more flexible than rubber. Just then, voices echo against the clear acrylic walls of a crystal corridor!

Turn to page 107.

Batman pulls on an oxygen mask and tank, and dives out of the Bat-Sub. *Good!* he thinks, as the Bat-Sub crashes into the teeth of the nuclear sub. *Their radar will show I crashed. They won't be expecting me!* He swims into the "whale's" gullet, slides down its "throat," and lands in a passageway outside the control room. One by one, he knocks out Scarecrow, Catwoman, Riddler, and the Joker, dragging each into a separate compartment and tying them up.

As the whale-sub heads for home, one of the freed millionaires asks, "Hey, where's Bruce Wayne?" Batman stammers: "Oh, er, he stayed on board the cruise ship. Don't worry, he's perfectly all right!"

The End

"There's a simple explanation, Two-Face!" shouts Batman, leaping up from the crowd and knocking the gun out of his hand. "Which one were you?" asks Two-Face. "You'll never know!" says Batman, quickly tying him up. "After your little show, I went around to all my fellow passengers and snapped them out of your hypnotic spell. Then I arranged a ruse so that each one would confess to being the real Batman! I thought that might confuse you just long enough for me to capture you. Now, come on, I've made up a nice little bed for you in the hold, until we reach dry land and you can take up residence in Gotham Penitentiary."

The End

Making sure everyone is holding on tight, Batman wraps his own arms around a mammoth molar. In pour tons of water and the remainder of the charity cruise passengers. "Batman!" cries one of them, grabbing a tooth. "Look! I think some enemy of yours knew you'd be on this cruise!" He is pointing to the roof of the whale's cavernous mouth. Embedded in the hard palate is some radio-controlled device. Batman acrobatically scurries up the inside of the jaw until he reaches the device. "A high-frequency brain alterator!" he exclaims. "I wondered what would make a peaceful animal like that whale attack us! See? The dial is set for 'HOSTILE ATTACK'!"

Unfortunately, the next setting on the dial is "SWALLOW AND DIGEST"!

The End

As soon as the Bat-Sub breaks the surface, Batman sees what happened. The whale-sub has crashed into the side of the enormous iceberg! But wait—what's this? All the millionaires are in life rafts! They must have escaped just before the crash—and they've captured the criminals!

"We took charge, Batman," says one of them. "It just made us so mad that here we were doing some good with our money, and these lousy crooks come along to do *harm* with it! Anyway, we short-circuited their radar equipment, once we found their emergency escape shuttlecraft!" One of the others looks sheepish. "We hope you don't mind, Batman!" But Batman is smiling. "Mind!" he says, looking at Riddler, Joker, Catwoman, and Scarecrow all tied up and soaking wet. "Not only don't I mind, gentlemen . . . I extend my heartiest congratulations. And thanks for helping me do my job!"

The End

I'd better be careful, thinks Bruce, rushing down to the lower deck lounge. *I don't want anyone to think Bruce Wayne is Batman.* He rips the fishnet decoration from the wall, runs to the railing, and throws it far out into the water. With perfect aim, he nets all the floundering millionaires and saves them from drowning. But just when everyone is safely back on deck, there is a terrible roaring sound from starboard. An enormous whale is speeding right toward the cruise ship! It will collide in seconds!

If Bruce changes into Batman, turn to page 86.

If he gets everyone below decks, turn to page 45.

Much later, when the villains have each gone to separate rooms, as Batman hoped, he sneaks over to the group of tied-up millionaires. "Shhh!" he says, laying a finger on his lips and untying them one by one. "We have some SABOTAGING to do! Come on! Let's find the control room for this floating fortress!" Batman finds the main engine room first, and goes over to the control panel. The fortress is on a course due north. *Probably to conceal themselves among the glacial mountains of the Arctic,* thinks Batman, *until they get the millionaires' money . . .* But Batman's thoughts are interrupted by gunshots, coming from deep within the acrylic mountain.

If Batman races off toward the sound of the shots, turn to page 69.

If he ignores the sounds just long enough to fiddle with the controls, turn to page 73.

Batman decides to play it safe and drive into one of the torpedo tubes concealed beneath the fins. *It's so quiet in here,* he thinks, once he has shut off his own engine. *The nuclear reactor has been shut down.* He steps out into the dry interior of the big fake whale, and right into a steel cage! "Ha ha!" roar the four criminals locking and surrounding the cage. "Too late, Batman," purrs the Catwoman. The Scarecrow pipes up triumphantly, "The President of the United States has given in to our ransom demands!" Joker and Riddler step aside to reveal the sad group of millionaires. "They get to go back home in disgrace," says Riddler, *"after we get our billion dollar payoff!"* giggles the Joker.

But the most fun, all four agree, will be delivering the great Batman—in a cage!

The End

Batman rushes to the police switchboard in the dispatch room. A quick search turns up a tiny computer concealed behind the switchboard. It is ingeniously wired to the transmitter and programmed with a vocal composite to sound just like Commissioner Gordon! As Batman examines it, suddenly it speaks: "It doesn't take a TRUNK CALL to find me, Batman!" Does the cryptic message have a meaning? Batman has a feeling he'd better act fast—this sounds like the Riddler!

If Batman runs back to the Batmobile and tries to solve the riddle, turn to page 96.

If he rushes up to the rooftop, turn to page 110.

For further information on the Riddler, turn to page 118.

Peering through a particularly clear chink in the wall, Batman sees that the millionaires are all tied up in a group. Talking to them are Riddler, Catwoman, Joker, and Scarecrow. So he can hear better, and to filter out the echoes, Batman places a tiny Bat-Amplifier in his ear. "This floating fortress," the Joker says, "is an ingenious war machine! Even Batman couldn't see through its camouflage!" Scarecrow leans forward. "We've banded together not only to defeat Batman, but to bring the world to its knees!" Now, Catwoman speaks up. "With your money and our cunning, we can rule the world!" Batman doesn't like the sound of THAT! He must do something.

If Batman attempts to capture all four at once, turn to page 116.

If he waits for an opportunity to trick them, turn to page 103.

Knowing the powerful echo effect in this floating fortress, Batman calls out, "ALL YOU MEN—ESCAPE NOW! REPORT IMMEDIATELY TO DOCKING PLATFORM AND WHALE-SUB!" Then, he runs to the sub himself as fast as he can, helps the last of the millionaires aboard, closes the hatch, and casts off.

"No, Riddler, no!" shrieks the Joker. "Stop firing! The gunshots will start a tremor! It's the only thing that can crack these acrylic walls—"

But it's too late. As Batman and the hostages escape in the camouflaged submarine to the safety of the open sea, the entire "ice" fortress comes crashing down on the heads of the cowering villains!

The End

Donning scuba gear, Batman ejects himself from the Bat-Sub. And not a moment too soon! As soon as he is clear of the craft, it suffers a direct hit by a whale-sub torpedo! Alone against the powerful nuclear submarine, Batman takes a small grenade from his utility belt and, diving suddenly, drops it in the fake blowhole of the camouflaged sub. As the explosion knocks out the sub's reactor that powers the craft, Batman watches the four villains emerge from the torpedo tubes beneath the fins with their captives—all wearing scuba gear. He swims around them, wrapping them in silken Bat-Rope. "Relax, everyone," says Batman when they reach the surface. "These four are going to tow us back to Gotham! Now, swim!"

The End

Batman swings to the rooftop and hides in the shadows, beneath the malfunctioning Bat-Signal. There he sees the Riddler, looking down with a pair of binoculars, and standing before a detonator. With a toss of the Batarang, the Caped Crusader clobbers the Riddler from behind. His cape swooping behind him, Batman grabs and disconnects the detonator, and puts the Riddler's wrists in Bat-Cuffs. "It was true that it didn't take a 'trunk call' to find you, Riddler! If I'd checked the Batmobile's trunk, you'd have set off a bomb hidden in it!" intones Batman. "The real clue to your hiding place was that sabotaged Bat-Signal! Once I rescue Gordon, you'll be telling punchlines to the other prisoners!"

The End

Shutting off his headlights in case he's driving into a trap, Batman steers blindly through the cave opening. *I can guide this trusty vessel by Bat-Radar!* thinks Batman. *It's the most sophisticated navigational instrument yet devised!* On the screen he can see that the giant whale-sub appears to be docked up ahead, right in the center of the iceberg! He slows to a dead halt and idles quietly for a few minutes before deciding to turn on the headlights. He floods the cave with light. The whale-sub *is* docked, its front end embedded in the ice wall, resembling a huge fish with its head stuck. *Now what?* thinks Batman.

If Batman steers his little sub right into the torpedo tube of the larger sub, turn to page 104.

If he aims for the ice wall, the same way the whale-sub did, turn to page 97.

Batman has seen a series of new wires running from the Transmission Tower to a fun house in the amusement park. Outside, a big mechanical clown laughs and shakes its sides. Inside, Batman finds the kidnapped Commissioner, tied up. The wires lead to a tape recorder. "Batman!" says the Commissioner. "That's not my voice! It belongs to him! And he's getting away!" Outside the window, the mechanical clown jumps off its pedestal. It's the Riddler, in disguise! Batman rips loose the recording wires and uses them to swing out the window, coming down with a crash squarely on the fleeing Riddler! "You should relax more, Riddler," says Batman, tying him up. "You were too wired!"

The End

Zigzagging wildly through the water, the tiny Bat-Sub attempts to outmaneuver the bigger craft, as lethal depth charges explode all around. KA-BOOOOM! *That one was close!* thinks Batman, turning his sub sharply around. *I've got to make for the underwater cave entrance!* Caught off guard momentarily, the four villains in the whale-sub watch on their radar screens, as the Bat-Sub disappears into the cave. "Ha ha ha!" laughs the Joker. "He just drove into the biggest BAT-TRAP ever devised! Ha ha!" Catwoman, Riddler, and Scarecrow all understand immediately. They torpedo the cave entrance, sending tons of solid ice down into the opening, sealing it for all eternity with Batman inside!

The End

Batman climbs the tower. At the very top, he hears the voice again, this time coming from the high-tension wires. "Out here! Please save me, Batman!"

Far below, standing by the switchbox, is the Riddler. He holds a tiny transmitter, sending over the wires the composite computer voice of Commissioner Gordon he had created to lure Batman to his death. The real Gordon isn't here at all! Just as the Riddler sees Batman crawling out on the wires, he throws the switch! There's a loud crackle, a flash of light, and down falls the unconscious Batman!

The End

Turning his Bat-Amplifier to full volume, Batman slips around the crystal wall and behind the villains. The startling sound of their own voices makes the villains turn in the direction of the Bat-Amplifier. Batman sees his chance and leaps into action! With three well-placed blows, Batman has knocked the Riddler, Scarecrow, and Joker out cold. But Catwoman gets away! When he turns around, Batman is surprised to see that the tied-up millionaires have tripped the escaping Catwoman with their feet, and sat on her! She is helplessly pinned beneath them!

"Good work!" laughs Batman, untying them. "Now, let's sail this camouflaged war machine back to the United States. It'll make a nice charitable donation to the U.S. Navy!"

The End

"Please!" cries Bruce Wayne, throwing his hands up in fear. "I'm not Batman!" Momentarily caught off guard by the millionaire's cowardly behavior, Two-Face's henchman forgets to pull the lever. At that instant, without stopping to change to Batman, Bruce leaps into the air with Olympic agility, spins once, and descends with a thrusting kick—propelling the flamethrowing camera out into the water. He knocks both crooks out cold. But the crowd is murmuring: "Can Bruce Wayne be Batman?"

After the police arrive, Bruce—now dressed as Batman—explains how he only pretended to be Bruce Wayne to capture whatever crook was threatening Batman. "Bruce Wayne," he adds, driving off in his Batmobile, "is really on the cruise!" And later that night, by means of an aqualung and hand-held Bat-Propellers, Batman does indeed join the cruise—as Bruce Wayne!

The End

Fact File

THE JOKER—Archenemy of Batman. He is a mad jester with a bizarre, fixed grin, who plays lethal jokes. Perhaps the cleverest and most dangerous of criminals.

THE RIDDLER—A criminal mastermind who has a pathological compulsion to tip Batman off to his crimes before committing them, by way of cryptic riddles.

TWO-FACE—Half-good, half-evil, Two-Face is half-handsome, half-ugly. He went mad after a chemical accident scarred half of his face.

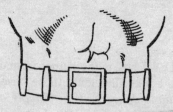

UTILITY BELT—An amazing miniature laboratory and tool kit. It has in late years been supplemented with numerous ingenious devices for emergency crimefighting, such as smoke bombs, many different types of Batarangs, grappling hooks, and flash powder.

BAT-SIGNAL—A searchlight with a bat emblem used by Commissioner Gordon to summon Batman in the event of an emergency.

RICHARD WENK is the author of many multiple choice books, including those based on the movie *Indiana Jones and the Temple of Doom*. He is a longtime Batman fan. Currently, he resides in California.

JOSE DELBO's comic book illustrations of the DC Comics Super Heroes are familiar to many people. Mr. Delbo is the artist for the daily Superman syndicated newspaper strip, and also does the artwork for the *Superman Sunday Special* newspaper puzzle page. He lives in New Jersey with his wife and two children.